The STICKY DOLL Trap

Jessica Souhami

F

FRANCES LINCOLN
CHILDREN'S BOOKS

I'm going to tell you a story
about that cheeky rascal, Hare.
And this is how it goes …

One long, hot summer when it didn't rain
for weeks, the sun dried up all the pools,
all the lakes and even the wide river.
The animals were very, very thirsty.
They scrabbled and scratched at the dry, dusty earth,
searching for water.

Well, everyone but that good-for-nothing Hare.
And where was he?

Hare was lying in the long grass!
"I'm not spoiling my pretty little paws
by digging in the dirt," he said.
And he shut his eyes and went to sleep.

At last, just before dusk, the animals' hard work
was rewarded. Clear, clean water bubbled up
from an underground spring. It tasted delicious!
"This precious water should be saved for
the animals who worked for it," said Monkey.
"I'll stand guard to keep thieves away."

So Monkey watched by the pool.
And, in the early morning…

along came Hare with an empty calabash!
"No water for you, Hare!" called Monkey.
But Hare just shut his eyes, dipped his paw
into the empty calabash, and licked it.
"Mmmm," he said. "Dee-licious!"

"What've you got there?" said Monkey. "Is it banana?"

"Better'n that!" said Hare.

"Is it mango?" said Monkey, looking hungry.

"Oh, better'n that!" said Hare.

"Is it **HONEY**?" said Monkey, his mouth watering.

"Much better'n that!" said Hare.

"Want to try some, Monkey? Open your mouth
 and shut your eyes and I'll give you a taste."

So Monkey opened his mouth and shut his eyes and waited for a taste of something wonderful. He waited and he waited – but no food came.

Meanwhile, that naughty Hare filled his calabash
with water and scampered away.

When poor Monkey opened his eyes he realised
how he had been tricked!

So the next day Hyena guarded the pool.
And very soon…

along came Hare with an empty calabash!
"No water for you, Hare!" shouted Hyena.
But Hare just shut his eyes, dipped his paw
into the empty calabash, and licked it.
"Mmmmm," he said. "Dee–licious!"

"What've you got there?" said Hyena. "Is it stew?"

"Better'n that!" said Hare.

"Is it roast chicken?" said Hyena longingly.

"Oh, better'n that!" said Hare.

"Is it **SAUSAGE**?" said Hyena, licking his lips.

"Much better'n that!" said Hare.

"Want to try some, Hyena? Open your mouth and shut your eyes and I'll give you a taste."

So Hyena opened his mouth and shut his eyes
and waited for a taste of something delicious.
And he waited and he waited – but no food came.

Meanwhile, that crafty Hare filled his calabash with water and fled.

When poor Hyena opened his eyes he realised how he had been tricked!

The next day, the angry animals made a plan
to catch that pesky Hare.
And this is what they did…

They collected gum from the rubber trees
and made a huge, gummy, sticky doll.
They set it by the water's edge,
hid behind a tree and waited.

And very soon…

along came Hare with his empty calabash.

"Hello," he said, surprised to see the doll.

"Who are you?

 Do you want a taste of something dee–licious?"

There was no reply.

"Are you rude or just asleep?"

Still no reply.

"I'LL WAKE YOU UP, ALL RIGHT!"

Hare slapped the doll with his right paw.
**AND HIS RIGHT PAW STUCK FAST
IN THE STICKY GUM!**

"Hey! That's not friendly!" Hare said.
He slapped the doll with his left paw.
AND HIS LEFT PAW STUCK FAST!

"Now, that's not nice!" he cried.
He kicked the doll with his right foot.
AND HIS RIGHT FOOT STUCK FAST!

"Ow! Let go!" he shouted.
He kicked the doll with his left foot.
AND HIS LEFT FOOT STUCK FAST!

"Just stop that!" he yelled.
He butted the doll with his head.
AND HIS HEAD STUCK FAST!

Now Hare was well and
truly trapped.

The animals gathered round, and pulled Hare off the sticky doll.

"We've got you now, you scoundrel!" said Monkey.

"But what shall we do with you?"

"Boil him!" said Hyena.

"Hang him!" said Hog.

"Roast him!" said Leopard.

But Hare didn't seem bothered at all.

"Oh yes!" he said. "**PLEASE** boil me, hang me, roast me
just as you like. But p-p-p-please, whatever you do,
p-p-p-please don't throw me into the spiny, thorny bushes."
And he began to shiver and shake all over.

The animals looked at each other.
"Well," they said, "if the bushes are that horrible,
that's exactly what we **WILL** do!"

So Monkey and Hyena picked up Hare
and with a one, and a two, and a three,
W-H-O-O-O-S-H-!
They threw him right into the middle
of the spiny, thorny bushes.

The animals waited and waited
to see what would happen.
And after a little while…

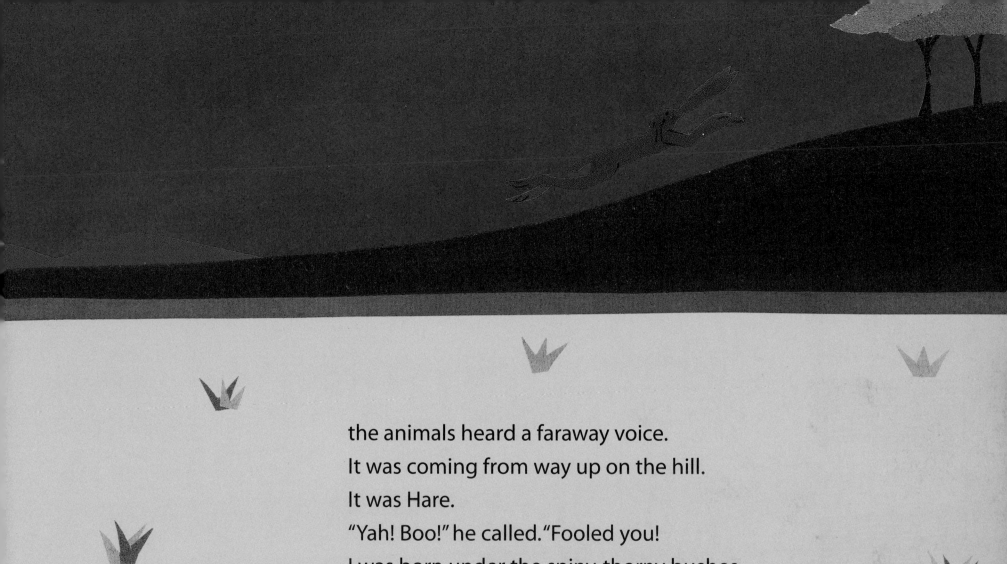

the animals heard a faraway voice.
It was coming from way up on the hill.
It was Hare.
"Yah! Boo!" he called. "Fooled you!
I was born under the spiny, thorny bushes.
I've lived all my life under the spiny, thorny bushes.
They can't hurt me!"
And he ran away laughing fit to burst.

And, I've been told, that cheeky rascal
is tricking and fooling everyone to this very day!
And that is the end of this story.

About the Story

The theme of catching a trickster with a sticky doll is a very old one.
The best-known version is the 'Uncle Remus' tale of Brer Rabbit and the Tar Baby.
This was written in the late 19th century by the white journalist, Joel Chandler Harris,
from the stories told by African slaves working on the cotton plantations
of the southern American states. But the story goes way back.
Those slaves carried the stories from their homelands; this story is told
all over South and West Africa, where the trickster is a hare,
the true ancestor of Brer Rabbit.

I have based my story on West African versions and, like all storytellers,
I have told the story in my own way.

First published in Great Britain in 2010 and in the USA in 2011 by
Frances Lincoln Children's Books, 4 Torriano Mews,
Torriano Avenue, London NW5 2RZ
www.franceslincoln.com

A catalogue record for this book is available from the British Library.

ISBN 978-1-84780-017-6

Illustrated with collage of Ingres papers hand-painted
with watercolour inks and graphite pencil

Set in Myriad

Printed in Shenzhen, Guangdong, China by C&C Offset Printing in March 2010

1 3 5 7 9 8 6 4 2